Seedlings

Fables from the Forest

by

C D Baker

DEDICATION

To Davy and Will; once Seedlings, now Trees

THIS BOOK BELONGS TO

_____

GREETINGS, SEEDLINGS!

Trees are the giants of the earth. They start off as little seedlings and then grow quickly....just like you.

Did you know that trees speak to each other when the wind moves through their branches? (This is a secret most humans don't know.) Well, they do, and when they talk to each other they love to tell stories.

The 'Wise Ones' tell the best stories because they are the oldest and have seen the most. These Wise Ones want to tell you some stories right now. So get ready, Seedlings! The winds are coming and the trees are about to speak.

BLUE SPRUCE

Deep in the northern wilderness lies the beautiful Snow Valley. Here the evergreen trees spread far and wide between the mighty mountains like a great green carpet.

There was a time when the most beautiful of all the evergreen trees was Blue Spruce. She was a tree of special color and shape. Her needles were silver-blue and every branch was perfect.

Douglas Fir was Blue Spruce's neighbor. He was a good tree. He liked Blue Spruce a lot but he felt sad for her. He knew that Blue was missing something.

"I know that I am beautiful," said Blue Spruce to Douglas one morning. "But I think I need something more."

Douglas Fir agreed. "Yes, Blue. You are missing something."

Blue looked at herself. She thought that her color was good, but maybe not good enough. "Ah...I see what I need. Say no more!"

So, Blue Spruce started doing everything she could to get more blue color into her needles. She dug her roots into new places, and she tried to get just the right sunshine.

A few years later, Blue waved a branch at Douglas. "I think I am bluer now. What do you think?"

Douglas answered. "Well, I guess you are a little more blue, but you are still missing something."

"I thought so!" cried Blue. "I know...I need to be bigger. Say no more!"

For the next years, Blue Spruce stretched her limbs toward the sky. She reached and strained, she groaned and moaned.

Finally, one day Douglas called out to her. "Blue...Blue! Listen to me."

"What, Douglas? I'm busy growing."

"Yes...but you are still missing something very important. Let me tell you what..."

"Ah!" said Blue. "Yes, I know what I need! I need more nests. Say no more!"

Blue Spruce spent months inviting every bird that flew near to make nests in her branches. "Come, come! I have the best branches of any tree in Snow Valley. Come, build your nests here!"

Come they did. Hundreds of birds crowded into the happy tree. Red birds and black birds came. So did brown ones and yellow. Birds of every color flew into Blue's blue branches. They brought their grasses and bits of bark, their twigs and their feathers. They decorated Blue with so many nests that she could feel their weight.

Blue was a little tired by now. "So, Douglas Fir, do you still think that I am missing something?"

Douglas answered sadly. "Yes. You are still missing something very important."

"Wait...wait!" shouted Blue in the wind. "I know. I need more cones. Say no more!"

Once again, the unsatisfied Blue Spruce worked day and night. This time she grew more and more cones. When autumn came, she had grown more cones than any tree in Snow Valley.

"What do you think, Douglas?" asked Blue.

Douglas Fir waited for a gentle breeze. When one came, he answered softly. "My friend, you really must listen to me. It's not important whether you are bluer, or bigger, or have more nests or more cones..."

"What?" Blue Spruce was suddenly angry. "What do you mean, 'not important?' I have worked hard to have what I have! Say no more!"

Douglas and Blue did not speak for the rest of that autumn. Before long, winter came to Snow Valley and the snows began to fall. By late January, the snow covered the evergreens with a heavy, white blanket.

By the middle of February, so much snow had fallen that Blue Spruce was suddenly afraid. Her white branches were already heavy from too many nests and cones...and now all this snow! They started to hurt.

At last, the exhausted Blue could no longer hold her branches. She strained and she struggled. One broke, and then another broke. Soon many broke and crashed to the ground.

Blue was very, very unhappy. She was afraid of what others were thinking. She wished she could hide, but all she could do was look down at the broken branches piled beneath her.

When spring came, the snow began to melt and Blue began to cry.

Douglas felt so sad for his friend. "Blue...Blue," he said. "Don't cry. You still have all of your friends. Look, there. Tall Pine is bending a 'hello'...and there, Old Larch is waving. The sun is warm and the sky is bright. You still have so much."

Blue Spruce said nothing.

Then Douglas decided it was time for him to say what he had wanted to say for a long time. "Listen, my friend. Now you *really* need what I wanted you to have all along."

"Oh, Douglas. I am so tired. I don't think I can do anything else." Blue Spruce sighed. "But go ahead, tell me what I need."

Douglas waited for just the right breeze. "All you ever really needed is a thankful heart."

Blue Spruce didn't answer at first. She looked at all the trees around her. She suddenly realized that they really did care about her.

Then she let the sunshine warm her. She listened to the birds that were singing to her.

Blue looked closely at Douglas Fir. "Oh dear Douglas," Blue said. "You are right. I do have more to be thankful for than I ever knew!"

Douglas was happy.

"Most of all," Blue said. "I am thankful that *you* are my friend. Thank you...and say no more, for now I understand."

Let your heart be filled with thankfulness.

from *Colossians 2:7*

Questions

1. Did you ever wish you had more of something?

2. Can you make a list of all the good things in your life?

3. How can we remember to be thankful?

4. What would you tell Blue Spruce?

Draw your own pictures, here!

SHADY MAPLE

One day, a brisk wind brought a group of twirling maple seeds to Springfield Flats. After some rain and warm sunshine, seedlings began to grow out of the ground. The first seedling to cast a tiny shadow was named, 'Shady Maple.'

Shady grew more quickly than the other seedlings. She liked that. She soon learned that if she grew the most leaves, she could have more to say. So, she hurried to grow leaves.

Shady also learned that if she could take the most soil with her roots, she could get the most water. So, she started to do that.

Then she learned that if she grew the biggest branches, she could take the most sunlight. So she did that, too.

As the seasons passed, Shady Maple kept growing bigger and bigger. She wanted to take as much as she could for herself. She liked the idea of having it all. She even thought she deserved it because she was the first to make shade.

But even though she had the most of everything, she became an angry tree. She didn't like it when her neighbors tried spreading their roots near hers. She didn't want them growing their branches too close, either.

One of her neighbors was Silver Maple. He began to complain. "Hey Shady," he said one day. "You need to share more root-room. I can barely get the food and water I need."

Shady didn't care. "That's too bad, Silver. I was here first. I deserve the most. But I'm not a mean tree. I've left everyone a little root-room. Just be thankful for that!"

Norway Maple wasn't happy, either. "You're shading me from the sun," he said. "You know that we can't grow leaves without sunlight. Can't you let me send a few of my branches through yours?"

"No," answered Shady. "I need all the light I can get. And if I let you do that, then all the others will try."

The wind blew and all the other Maples complained loudly. "You're so selfish," they shouted. But Shady Maple didn't care what they thought. She didn't care about them at all.

The years passed and then things got worse. One day, Shady made an announcement. "Listen, everyone. I need *more* root-room."

"More! Your roots are everywhere!" the others shouted.

"I have tried to be generous," Shady said. "But I have so many leaves that I need more water and food for them. You are all smaller. You will just have to grow your roots somewhere else."

"But where?" asked Silver Maple. He was suddenly scared. "You spread your roots all the way past mine."

"Yeah!" complained Norway. "See, you *are* mean!"

"No, I am *not* a mean tree." Shady thought for a moment. "I have an idea. You can grow your roots *under* my roots." She was happy with her idea. "Yes, that's it. I'll take the soil on top and all of you can have whatever you want down deep."

"No!" shouted Silver. "That's not fair!"

Norway Maple was not happy about this idea. "The deep soil is too hard to dig through. Why should you get all the soft soil on top?"

But Shady was too big for them to stop. "That's the way it will be," she said. "I deserve to have what I have. Remember, I was the first to make shade."

So, for the next years, Shady Maple kept on spreading her shallow roots far and wide across the grove. She drew all the water from the soft top soil and shared none of it with the others.

At the same time, her poor neighbors struggled to dig their roots deeper and deeper into the hard ground underneath.

One June, however, the sun seemed hotter than usual. The spring rains had ended early. Shady had to pull harder on her roots for a drink.

By July, Springfield Flats was in bad shape. No rain had fallen for a very long time. That's when Shady Maple knew she was in big trouble.

Shady was very thirsty. Her leaves started to turn from green to yellow. Her many roots were long, but she had only grown them in the soil on top. That soil was now the driest soil of all.

"You're getting sick," said Silver in a dry wind.

Shady could only whisper an answer. "I *am* sick."

The middle of August came and still there was no rain on Springfield Flats. The soil was now dry and cracked. Shady was very, very weak. "Silver, Norway...can you help me?" she said. "Can you cast a little shade over me? Please?"

The other Maples stared at their selfish neighbor. She had taken every drop of water from the top soil. They were thirsty, too. But they were not as sick as Shady. That's because their roots were deep in the ground where there was still a little water.

Silver Maple answered Shady. "You wouldn't help us, remember?"

Shady stayed quiet.

"You wanted the soil on top and all the sunlight. You said that you deserved to have everything you have."

Shady was silent for a very long time. Then she finally answered. "You are right, Silver. I always thought I deserved everything I have." Shady became very sad. "Now I have exactly what I deserve."

Silver and Norway thought about Shady. Finally, Silver spoke to Norway. "Shady is mean, but I think she's sorry."

"Well, I guess..." said Norway.

"Now look at her," said Silver. "She is still one of us. We have to try and help. I just hope it's not too late."

Norway agreed. "What if we all stretched our roots? Do you think we could push some water toward her?"

Silver wasn't so sure about the idea. "That's never been done..."

"But we could try," said Norway.

A sudden, cool breeze blew through the trees. Silver began to shout, happily. "Look up, Shady! Everyone, look up!"

Shady Maple looked up. The sky was filling with clouds. Rain was coming to Springfield Flats! It would soon fall on those who deserved it...and those who did not.

'At last!' Shady said. Then she looked at her neighbors. "After all my selfish ways, you were going to help me. Now I want to be different." She was excited. "When I am healthy again, I promise that I will share everything with you!"

The rain started to fall. Shady Maple and her friends drank and drank and drank. It rained for weeks. When the sun came out again, all the trees were green.

Shady was now happy and healthy. In the years that followed, she kept her promise. All her friends learned to love her, and Shady Maple was never selfish again.

Be kind to one another; Be gentle and forgiving. From Ephesians 4:32

Questions

1. Are you sometimes selfish?

2. How can we learn to share what we have with others?

3. How can we forgive people who take things from us?

PROUD POPLAR

On a warm spring day, a noisy bird dropped two seeds on the sunny side of Gusty Ridge. One was from a Mulberry tree and the other from a Poplar tree. Soon, the seeds made roots and seedlings began to sprout.

   After a few good summers, the two seedlings had grown just enough leaves to whisper to each other in the steady winds of the ridge. They quickly became the best of friends. Together they watched over the beautiful valley below.

   Seasons passed and the trees grew. But one summer afternoon Poplar looked down at his friend, Mulberry. "Hey, Mulberry," he rustled. "You aren't keeping up with me. I've grown much taller than you."

   "That's okay," answered Mulberry. "I'll try and catch up."

So, for the next years Mulberry tried hard to grow as fast as Poplar. He stretched his limbs and tried lifting his trunk, but nothing seemed to work. Finally, Mulberry called to Poplar. "Can you hear me up there?"

Poplar answered, "Yes."

"I'm worried," said Mulberry. "I can't grow much. What should I do?"

"I don't know but I wish you would do something," said Poplar. "You look silly. You're short and you're fat and your branches are all crooked. Your leaves are ugly and your berries make a mess."

Poplar's words made Mulberry feel very sad.

Then Poplar said something even more unkind. "I think I'll start growing my branches over top of you so nobody will see how awful you look."

Before long, Poplar did just what he said. Poplar soon became everyone's favorite. People came from the village to have picnics under his huge branches.

The butterflies loved Proud Poplar, too. And the birds perched all over him and sang him songs. But the birds laughed at Mulberry. They dropped their seed shells and feathers on top of him from Poplar's branches.

One afternoon, Poplar announced to everyone that he was a very amazing tree. "In fact," Proud Poplar said, "from where I stand, I don't see another tree more beautiful than me."

Mulberry mumbled back. "Yes, Poplar, you are very special."

Proud Poplar laughed. "I am so glad that I don't look like you, Mulberry! You get uglier every year. You're lucky you can hide in my shadow."

Mulberry was too hurt to answer, but he worried about his friend.

One day Mulberry heard some thunder. "You know, Poplar," he said. "If you get too tall the lightning will hit you."

A week later, the sky began to change. A strange color filled the air.

Proud Poplar watched his birds fly away. He looked up to see the sky turning purple and black. "I'm...I'm...scared," Poplar said, slowly. "I've never been scared before."

"I'm scared, too," answered Mulberry. The two trees knew that something bad was going to happen.

Then, angry clouds began to race toward Gusty Ridge. A sudden blast of wind howled into the two trees. Lightning flashed. Thunder crashed.

"This is not good!" cried Poplar.

Mulberry answered, "No...not...good! Be careful up there!"

Huge raindrops started to beat against the trembling trees. The wind blew hard. Proud Poplar's limbs began to shake, wildly.

"Poplar! Poplar? Can you hear me?" cried Mulberry.

"Help me!" shouted Poplar. "The wind is too strong for me!"

Poplar's leaves began to tear off. His big trunk was bending over and starting to crack.

Mulberry gripped the soil with his roots, tightly. He held on to his branches with all the strength that he had.

And then it was over.

Gusty Ridge became still and quiet. The sun popped out from behind the clouds.

The exhausted Mulberry looked around at his wet, battered branches. "Wow. I'm still here." Then he saw his friend. "Oh no!"

Poor Poplar had been broken. Not much was left of him. "Oh, Mulberry, it hurts," Poplar said. "Look at me."

Mulberry felt so sad for him. At first, he didn't know what to say. He could only stare at poor Poplar.

Finally he said, "Well, you are still alive..."

"Alive? Look at me!" said Poplar. "What do I do now?"

"Well, you can listen to me," said Mulberry. "As long as you are alive, you always have hope."

Poplar wiggled his roots.

"You can start growing again...now," said Mulberry. "And even though I'm short, I am wide enough to protect you until you can take care of yourself."

Poplar did not answer all that day or all that night. When the morning came, he looked over at his stubby friend and said, "Thank you, Mulberry. I'm very sorry for the way I looked down on you. You're the one who is special."

Mulberry was embarrassed.

Then Poplar said, "I'd like to grow with you again. And I want to be a better friend."

Mulberry smiled.

The years passed and the broken Poplar did grow again. Though he was never quite the same, he was a happier tree. He and Mulberry spent many good days sharing the sun, the butterflies and the birds, and talking to each other in the big winds of Gusty Ridge.

Don't be proud, but think of others more than yourself.

from *Philippians 2:3*

Questions

1. Is it ever okay to feel special?

2. How do others feel when we act like we are more important than they are?

3. Is everybody valuable in their own way?

4. What would you like to tell Mulberry?

SLOPE-OAK

The quiet waters of Mudbottom Creek wandered gently through a sleepy forest. Here, great oaks and shaggy hickory trees made a peaceful home for squirrels and rabbits and other forest friends.

One of the oak trees was named 'Slope-Oak' because he grew on steep slope by the water. Slope-Oak was very lazy. He never wanted to work hard like the rest of his Oak family. He liked the easy sunlight that his leaves could take from the open space above the water. He also liked the easy water that his roots could draw from the creek.

Grandfather Oak warned him that he should not grow so close to the edge. He told him to try and grow away from the water. "It's hard, I know," said the wise old Oak. "But you'll be stronger if you dig this way instead of that..."

But Slope-Oak wouldn't even try. He liked easy things.

One day, the fuzzy caterpillars told the trees that a terrible winter was coming. The Wise Ones of the forest then made an announcement. "Attention all trees! We must help the animals every way we can!"

"Did you hear that, Slope-Oak?" said Shagbark Hickory. Shagbark was Slope-Oak's neighbor. "We all need to do something. We Hickory's can make more nuts. You Oaks can make lots of acorns..."

"Oh no," yawned Slope-Oak. "My family works hard, but I don't."

"You won't help the animals? Don't you care?"

Slope-Oak shrugged and yawned again. "I care, but that's a lot of work. I'm sure something easier will come up."

For the next months, grateful squirrels were busy harvesting hickory nuts and acorns from the hard-working trees...except for Slope-Oak. He never bothered making very many.

"Slope-Oak!" said his grandfather. "The animals need your help. What kind of Oak are you?"

"Oh, I'll help," answered Slope-Oak.

Winter was cold that year. The trees could not remember ever seeing so much snow.

One day, Shagbark Hickory creaked his branches and said, "Look at these poor creatures, Slope-Oak. They need more food. How can we help?"

Slope-Oak watched a mother squirrel dig hard for nuts beneath the deep snow. Her children were hungry and too weak to move. Slope-Oak felt bad for the squirrels, but what could he do now?

Then the creek froze. Slope-Oak thought that was good news. "You see, Shagbark," he said. "Now the strong ones can go get food on the other side. Then they can bring it back over here for the weak ones." Slope-Oak felt better. "Nobody had to work so hard after all."

Winter ended suddenly that year. The ice melted quickly. It all happened so fast that many of the forest creatures were now trapped on the far side.

Slope-Oak watched them, carefully. They wanted to come home but couldn't. He felt very sad for them.

And then things got worse. Heavy rains began to crash atop the forest. Mudbottom Creek got higher and higher. The brown water churned and rolled. Rocks began to break away from the banks.

Slope-Oak suddenly became very nervous for himself. The rising water was rushing closer and closer to him. Finally, one dark night he could feel the dirt around his roots breaking loose. He felt himself slipping. "Help me, Shagbark!" he cried. "Help!"

"What can I do?" shouted his friend.

Slope-Oak began to tip over. "I'm falling! Help me!"

Shagbark couldn't help him. Nobody could help him. Without deep roots in good soil, poor Slope-Oak could not hold on. He tilted, then slid, and finally crashed across Mudbottom Creek with a terrible cry.

When dawn came, all the trees could see what happened to Slope-Oak. They were surprised. Instead of washing away, Slope-Oak now lay across the creek like a bridge.

Poor Slope-Oak was confused and scared. He was also suddenly sorry for his lazy ways.

Then he heard his grandfather's voice. "Be brave, Slope-Oak. You still have a few roots holding over here."

It was true. He was still attached to the bank...though barely. Grandfather Oak cried out again. "If you're willing to work like the Oak you are, start sending your roots deep into this side. If you can get a good hold, you could be a very strong bridge for a very long time!"

Slope-Oak lay there all that night and thought about what his grandfather said. He was certainly glad that he had not washed away. But did he want to be a bridge?

Morning came and squirrels, rabbits, deer, and the other friends of the forest scrambled toward Slope-Oak. They now had a way to go home!

Slope-Oak could feel their paws and feet scrambling happily over him. He could even hear them thanking him as they raced back to their families.

Slope-Oak suddenly liked his grandfather's idea. "Yes," he said. "Yes, I *will* be a bridge..."

The trees of Mudbottom Creek cheered for him.

Slope-Oak was happy. It felt better to help others than he expected.

Over the years that followed, Slope-Oak worked hard to dig his roots deep into the bank. It was not easy, but Slope-oak learned to love his work, and the grateful animals loved him for it. Eventually he became a very strong bridge...and was one for a very long time.

"Humbly serve one another in love."

from *Ephesians 4:2*

Questions

1. What does it mean to be 'lazy?"

2. How does being lazy hurt other people?

3. How does being lazy hurt you?

4. What would you like to say to Slope-Oak?

THE GARDEN BEECH

A kind gardener saved enough money to buy a house for his family. He was excited to plant a new garden with his young son.

One sunny morning, the gardener and his son carried some very special seedlings to the new garden. The gardener looked across the large, empty space. "There, son," he pointed. "On the north side we will plant the Holly tree because she can handle the cold winds."

The gardener turned. "To the east we will plant the Japanese Maple. That way she can look toward her home. "

The gardener turned again. "There...on the south side we will plant the Magnolia tree to remind us of the beauty of warm places."

The gardener turned one last time. "On the west side we will plant the Pear tree. That way we can pick her fruit in the last light of the day."

Then the gardener picked up the last seedling. He walked to the very center of the garden. "And here is where we will plant my favorite tree of all...my beautiful Beech tree."

The gardener and his son carefully planted the seedlings. When they were done, they smiled.

"Someday, son," the gardener said, "maybe you and your children or your grandchildren will walk through this garden. You can tell them of this day. Maybe you will have a picnic under my Garden Beech!"

During the next years, the gardener and his son tended the seedlings carefully. They trimmed and watered them with love and care. The young trees grew in the good garden soil. Soon they became strong saplings.

Then one sad day, the gardener got very bad news. He had to leave his house and abandon the garden that he loved.

Years passed and the young trees grew up behind the crumbling house with no one to care for them.

One wintry afternoon, a cold wind blew through the lonely garden. Garden Beech grumbled to Holly Tree. "I am planted in the middle where I'm closed in by everyone. I wish I stood where you do, Holly."

Holly answered. "You always want what others have. You're in the middle because you were the gardener's favorite tree. You are *special*!"

"Don't mock me, Holly Tree," fluttered Beech. "You know you are better than I am. Your leaves stay green in winter when mine are all gone. I wish that I could stay green like you."

"I wasn't mocking you!" answered Holly.

The two trees argued all day long. Finally, Beech said, "I am going to stop growing leaves on your side of me, Holly! That way I never have to speak to you again!"

And that's exactly what Garden Beech did.

The next spring, Japanese Maple whispered to Beech. "I hope you know that you look silly with no buds on one side."

Beech became angry. "Of course you think I look silly. You're beautiful. You have curvy branches and lacy leaves. I wish I looked like you!"

Japanese Maple answered, "But you are a wonderful tre..."

Beech interrupted. "Don't make fun of me. I'm going to tangle my branches with yours. Then you won't be so pretty!"

Many more years passed. Holly Tree and Japanese Maple were very unhappy...and so was Beech.

Then, one hot summer day Magnolia finally dared to say something. "Beech, you are a bully!"

Garden Beech answered, angrily. "Bully? You listen to me, Magnolia. It's easy for you to be gentle and sweet. You are covered in white flowers that smell good. I wish I had flowers like that!"

"But there's nothing wrong with you," answered Magnolia. She was suddenly scared.

Beech thought for a moment. "Since you're so mean, I don't want to smell you anymore. I will grow my branches over you and take your sunlight. Then you won't be able to grow flowers ever again! "

And so he did.

The seasons continued to come and go. One autumn evening, Beech decided to study Pear Tree.

"You have lots of pears this year," said Beech. "I think you are a show-off."

"I...I...I'm not showing off," said the nervous Pear. "You make shade, I make fruit. It's just what each of us do."

Garden Beech became very angry. "I wish I had fruit!" He waited for a powerful gust of wind and then shouted, "It's not fair! From now on I am going to move my bugs and worms over here and shake them on you."

Many more summers came and many winters went. The once beautiful Garden Beech had become a horrible site. His one side was bare and another was tangled. One side was overgrown and another was full of bugs and worms.

Beech soon realized that this was all very wrong. He had made his neighbors miserable and he was very,

very unhappy. He didn't know what to say anymore, but the others heard him crying in the rain.

Finally, one warm August morning an old man came into the garden with a curious child. "Where are we, Pop Pop?" asked the little girl.

The old man took off his hat. He was sad. He stood silently for a moment. "I helped my father plant this garden when I was a little boy." He looked around at the tall weeds and the neglected trees. "Now I bought it for us."

The girl took his hand. "Oh, Pop Pop...We can make the garden beautiful again. I promise! We can pull out all the weeds and plant new flowers..."

The old man walked quietly toward Garden Beech. He remembered how much his father loved this tree. He laid his hands on Beech's smooth bark. "What about this tree?" He wiped his eyes. "I think we'll have to cut it down..."

"No!" The little girl ran to Beech. "No, Pop Pop, we can save him...I know it." She hugged Garden Beech's wide trunk.

"Do you really think we can?" Pop Pop asked.

"Yes!" the girl answered.

So the old man quickly hired good gardeners who worked very hard. They fed and watered all the flowers and trees. They had to cut off lots of Beech's bad branches. That hurt Beech a little, but it helped him a lot.

When the work was done, the old man, the little girl, and all the gardeners enjoyed a picnic. "The garden is so beautiful, Pop Pop!" said the little girl. "Look at the pretty flowers and nice grass," she clapped. "And look at the trees! They must be very happy!"

The old man smiled. "Yes, it is all very beautiful," he said. Then the old man stood close to Garden Beech. He looked up. "And I think that *this* tree is now the happiest tree of them all."

Loving kindness changes hearts.

from *Romans 2:4*

Questions

1. Do you know a bully? Are you ever a bully?

2. Do you think most bullies are happy?

3. Bullies think they are strong, but what's the most powerful force in the world?

4. Do you think Garden Beech learned his lesson?

THE END

C. David Baker writes full-time from his small farm in Bucks County, Pennsylvania where he and his wife raise livestock with an interest in natural and humane methods. The father of two sons, he has written seven historical novels and two books of Christian reflection, which have been variously published in the U.S., U.K., Ukraine, Germany, Belarus, and Russia. *Seedlings* is his first children's book. Baker has a Master's degree in theology from the University of St. Andrews, Scotland.

More information is available at: www.cdbaker.com

Made in the USA
Middletown, DE
26 July 2022

69841341R00033